About the Author

Ethan Daniel James is the creator and host of the highly popular YouTube channel THE HONEST CARPENTER. A lifelong carpenter and tradesman, he now spends much of his time writing and teaching people how to work with their hands. He lives in Greensboro, North Carolina.

Visit the author at:
www.edanieljames.com
www.youtube.com/c/thehonestcarpenter

DungeonWorld

#1: One Hot Spark
#2: The Big Whiff
#3: Bang the War Drum
#4: The Royal Mess
#5: The Ghoul Ranch

DUNGEON WORLD

E. DANIEL JAMES

THE BIG WHIFF

This is a work of fiction. Names, characters, places, and incidents either are the product of the author's imagination or are use fictitiously. Any resemblance to actual persons, living or dead, events, or locales is entirely coincidental.

Copyright © 2022 by E. Daniel James

All rights reserved. No part of this book may be reproduced or used in any manner without written permission of the copyright owner except for the use of quotations in a book review.

First paperback edition 2022

Book Illustrations by Michelle Nobles

ISBN 978-1-957349-02-2 (paperback)

ISBN 978-1-957349-03-9 (ebook)

Honest Carpenter Publishing

Visit the author online!

www.edanieljames.com

THE BIG WHIFF

E. Daniel James
Illustrated by Michelle Nobles

1. Ogre Anger

Have you ever tried to argue with an ogre? Well, *don't!*

They're bossy, stubborn, and rude. Also, they have huge horns on their heads, and their breath smells like burning tires!

You'd have to be a total dunce to argue with an ogre.

And yet, that's exactly what I was doing on my second lousy afternoon in Dungeonworld.

"Sewer duty!" I shouted. "You can't put me on sewer duty!"

"Oh yeah?" Thoracks growled. "Says who?"

"Says *me.*"

"Well, last time I checked, you weren't the

boss around here. I'm the boss! So, I reckon you'll do what I tell you!"

Thoracks was as big and scary as ogres came. He had blue skin, bulging muscles, and a reputation for eating people who made him mad. He was the last monster you wanted to argue with.

But what choice did I have?!

He was talking about sending me to work in

the Big Whiff—the Dungeonworld sewer. All because I had made one little mistake in the blacksmith shop. I had to at least put up a fight!

"This is so *unfair*," I whined.

"Unfair? You blew up the dang smithy!"

"I didn't blow it up. I just sort of…burned it to the ground."

Thoracks grappled the air with his huge paws.

"Big difference! It'll take weeks to get it built back up. And you weren't hardly there an hour!"

He was technically right about that. I had only been working in the blacksmith shop for all of thirty minutes before I'd caused a huge flood and fire. But it wasn't my fault!

The head blacksmith—a hot-tempered ogre named Redbone—made me work too fast stoking the forge. I sort of blew hot ash everywhere. Then a clumsy troll got involved. One thing led to another and, well…*kaboom!*

Bye-bye, smithy.

Thoracks stomped around his cave-like

office, rubbing his clawed fingers against his blue forehead.

"Spark," he snorted. "I should've named you *Spike*...cause you're like a needle in my hairy rump!"

Spark is the name Thoracks gave me when I first showed up in Dungeonworld. To tell you the truth, I sort of liked the name. And Thoracks could be a pretty decent guy, too—when he didn't have smoke puffing out of his nostrils.

I thought I could soften him up a little.

"Come on, Thoracks," I said. "I'm sorry about what happened. *Really*."

"Ha! I'm supposed to believe that?"

"Honest!" I said. "I feel just terrible. The guilt is eating me up!"

Thoracks twisted his cow lips. He crossed his big, muscled arms.

"I'm not convinced," he said.

I gritted my teeth.

I'm not the type to play the pitiful card. It's just not my style. But if I was going to get out of this one, I knew I would have to put on a real show. A category-five guilt trip. So, I dug deep and turned on the waterworks.

"Please, Thoracks," I whimpered. "I-I-I didn't mean to ruin everything. It was just an accident. If you let me off the hook this time, I *promise* it won't ever happen again."

My lips quivered and shook. A solemn teardrop rolled down my cheek.

It was quite a performance!

And for a moment, it seemed like it just might work. Thoracks' ugly blue face relaxed. He uncrossed his arms and shuffled his hooves awkwardly.

"Really?" he asked.

I nodded sadly.

"*Really.*"

Thoracks sighed. His voice became calm and gentle.

"You're right," he said. "I reckon it won't

ever happen again…because you'll be mucking out swamp pipes down in the Big Whiff!"

He burst into barking laughter, rattling the pictures on the walls around us.

My crocodile tears dried right up.

"*Bull-faced butthead!*" I said.

But Thoracks didn't even hear me. He was too busy crowing and strutting around the room.

"Yessirree, I reckon you'll fit right in down in the Big Whiff. All the worst stuff sinks to the bottom down there!"

He pulled a rope cord by his desk. A bell rang.

The Big Whiff

"Fetrol, get in here!"

The wooden door to the office swung open. A tall, slightly rotten ghoul came limping in. His tattered clothes were held together with frayed rope, and he smelled like a moldy basement.

"You raaang, sir?"

"Spark here just earned himself an eon working sewer duty," Thoracks said. "Send him down to the Big Whiff, pronto…and see to it that he gets there!"

Fetrol's runny eyes widened.

"Right away, sir…"

He grabbed me by the elbow and began dragging me out of the room.

"You've really done it this time, young man," he hissed into my ear. "Come on before he changes his mind and eats you!"

Then the door shut behind us. And my fate was sealed.

2. Another Fine Mess

Out in the hallway, we were instantly surrounded by ogres, goblins, and trolls of all shapes and sizes. They were lumbering in every direction—jostling, jolting, and shouting at one another.

Just a typical afternoon in Dungeonworld.

And what is Dungeonworld, exactly?

Imagine an underground kingdom full of fire, steel, and stone. There's no electricity, no sunlight. Human kids are kept as servants known as "brunts," and the whole place is run by selfish, angry monsters.

Yep. That's where I live.

How did I wind up down here?

The same way every brunt does, I guess. I

opened a door called MORTAL PERIL and got snatched by two nasty goblins. They sized me up and tossed me down a dark hole. I fell for what felt like an eternity.

When I finally hit the bottom, Dungeonworld was waiting for me.

Whoopee.

The crazy thing is, I actually sort of liked it down here.

There were caverns and waterfalls galore!

Bridges and bats and bonfires! Adventure lurking around every corner! I could have been spending every minute exploring to my heart's content.

But *nooo...*

In Dungeonworld, they make you *work* all the time. And *clean* all the time. Two of the things I hate the most. And now, I was going to have to do both in the worst place imaginable...*the Big Whiff.*

It was a total nightmare!

Apparently, Fetrol felt the same way because he shook his head and tisked as we hurried down a series of hallways.

"It's really a bit harsh if you ask me. Thoracks hasn't sent anyone down to the Big Whiff in ages. Not since the last fellow died of the stench!"

"Is it really *that* bad, Fetrol?" I asked anxiously.

He looked down at me with his runny-egg eyes.

"This is Dungeonworld, Spark. Our sewer

is not a pretty sight. Just imagine what sort of stuff gets flushed around here!"

I did. And the thought made me very queasy.

"You don't think you could let me off the hook, do you, Fetrol? I mean, you could just *tell* Thoracks you sent me down to the Big Whiff. I'd lay low for a while. He would never know the difference!"

Fetrol laughed a big puff of dust.

"Ha! Thoracks knows everything that happens around here, young man. If I disobeyed him, he'd send me right down there with you. I'll just do my job, thank you very much."

The Big Whiff

"Some friend you are!" I spat.

A gobliness passed by carrying a raven in a rusty cage. We were going so fast I bumped right into her.

"Watch out!" she screeched. "Don't ruffle her feathers!"

"Don't ruffle mine, lady!" I shouted back.

"Come, come!" Fetrol said. "We'd best beat the rush."

"Where are we going anyways?" I asked.

"To the Shakylegs," Fetrol said. "You'll want a hot drink before you go."

The Shakylegs was the rowdiest tavern in all of Dungeonworld. It seemed like a strange place to go at the moment. But if it kept me out of the Big Whiff a minute longer, I was all for it.

We walked through a long, low tunnel and came out in the Pit.

This was a wide-open space that looked

like a huge indoor mall with a hundred levels. Countless torches flickered in the gloom up above, and bats swooped and swirled through the musty air.

A spiral walkway circled the entire Pit. Fetrol pulled me by the wrist, and we began running up it.

We zipped by arches and doorways where ghouls moaned and ogres groaned. We darted by caves packed with big, gray trolls juggling rocks.

We even passed by a little notch in the wall with a dirty yellow curtain over it. Not a soul was inside.

That's because I lived there.

"Can I stop by home real quick?" I asked.

"Best not," Fetrol said. "You might be tempted to sit down and rest!"

"That was kind of the point…" I muttered.

He continued pulling me right along.

Up and up we went, winding around the pavilion far below. Finally, we stopped in front of a particularly dank room with torches glowing inside. The sign over the door said THE SHAKYLEGS.

Normally, there would have been two huge trolls guarding the door. But it was afternoon, and the place wasn't busy yet. Fetrol thrust me forward.

"In you go, then!"

3. Pepper Soda

A BLONDE LADY OGRE was building a house of cards on the stone countertop when we walked in. She looked up and smiled as we slipped between the wooden benches and rickety tables.

"Sparky! Fetrol! You're in awful early."

"Hey, Caledonia," I grumbled.

Caledonia was my first friend in Dungeonworld. She was as nice as ogres came, and she gave me my pickled onions for free. She must have seen the glum look on my face as I climbed onto a stool.

"What gives, Sparky? You look like a troll who just stepped in dung."

"I feel more like the dung than the troll," I told her.

Fetrol flicked a strand of bat hair off my shoulder.

"He had a bit of a mishap in the blacksmith shop today," he said.

Caledonia gasped.

"Blimey! So, *you're* the one who burned down the smithy?"

I glanced up sharply.

"You already know?"

"Word gets around fast in Dungeonworld, kid."

"*Great…*"

I plopped my elbows onto the counter and sank my chin onto my folded arms. Caledonia looked me over.

"I don't see no teeth marks on you. I guess Thoracks didn't try to take a bite outta you then?"

"No, no. Thoracks is doing far worse than

that," Fetrol said. "He's sending Spark down to the Big Whiff!"

Caledonia's hands jolted so badly she knocked down her house of cards.

"Crum! You're joking!"

"Afraid not," Fetrol replied.

"Blimey…I wouldn't be caught dead down there," Caledonia said. "I've heard the smell alone can knock down a suit of armor!"

I groaned loudly and sank even further.

"You're not helping, Cal!"

"Sorry, Sparky..."

Fetrol patted me on the shoulder.

"I thought we could give him a *nice hot drink* before we send him on his way."

Caledonia thumped the counter with a fist.

"I've got just the thing for you…*pepper soda*."

Caledonia reached under the counter and pulled out a glass bottle with red liquid inside.

She popped the metal top with her yellow thumbnail and set it in front of me.

I eyed the bottle suspiciously. Bubbles were simmering inside.

"What's pepper soda?" I asked.

"A real eye-opener! Fizzy soda brewed with the spiciest funk peppers around. Go on, give it a sniff."

Experimentally, I put my nose over the top and took a whiff.

"Wowza!"

It was like someone had blown volcano fumes up my nostrils! My sinuses began to tingle. My eyes started to water. I had to yank my head back and sneeze.

"I don't know about that, Cal," I said.

"Come on. Don't be a milksop. Bottoms up!"

I sat there rubbing my chin.

I'm not one to chicken out very often. And if it was going to help get me ready to go into the Big Whiff, I thought I might as well give it a try. So, I held my breath, put the bottle to my lips, and tipped it back…

Gulp.

It was like swallowing fire!

Flames shot down my throat. Hot vapors poured from my nose. Lava tears squirted from my eyes. I slammed the bottle back down and had a full-blown coughing fit.

"Ack! Ick! Ock!"

I erupted like a muffler on a diesel truck. Actual black smoke came out of my mouth!

"That's the ticket!" Caledonia said.

When I finally managed to open my eyes again, everything was red for a moment.

"How do you feel?" Fetrol asked.

"Actually," I wheezed. "A little better…"

He pulled out an hourglass on a rope and looked at it. His eyebrows rose.

"That's good…because it's high time I sent you on your way!"

4. The Muckbucket

"Caledonia, can we use your Muckbucket?" Fetrol asked.

Caledonia grimaced.

"I reckon you'd better..."

We slid off our stools and followed her behind the counter.

"What's a muckbucket?" I asked nervously.

"You'll just have to see for yourself, Sparky."

We walked through a swinging door into a cluttered, musty room. A big sink against the wall was full of dishes and gray soap suds. Pots and pans hung everywhere. Huge jars of pickled onions and moldy mushrooms lined the shelves.

"This is the kitchen," Caledonia said. "And *that's* the muckbucket."

She pointed to what looked like a stone wishing well in the corner. Flies were buzzing around it. A wooden lid sat crookedly on top.

Caledonia pulled the lid off to reveal a hideous brown goo stewing inside. Mysterious lumps and chunks floated on the surface. I could see bones and fur, bits of rotten vegetables. The whole thing smelled like a dumpster rotting in the sun!

"Ugggh! It's like an awful compost heap," I said.

"That's exactly what it is," Caledonia replied. "All the scraps from the tavern get tossed in here. Whatever doesn't get eaten, we just pull this chain and send it down to the Big Whiff."

I pinched my nose.

"Totally wretched."

I waited for her to put the lid back on. But she didn't. Instead, she and Fetrol just stood there looking at me.

Her words slowly sank in.

"Wait, you're not telling me…"

"Afraid so," Fetrol said.

I couldn't believe what I was hearing.

"I'm not letting you flush me down that thing!" I sputtered.

"It's the fastest way to the Big Whiff, Sparky," Caledonia said. "Unless you'd rather take the troll toilet down."

"I'd rather not take *anything* down!"

"You really don't have much of a choice," Fetrol said. "Thoracks gave orders."

Orders schmorders! I thought.

I crossed my arms. Planted my feet wide.

"I won't do it," I said flatly. "You can't make me."

Fetrol sighed.

"I was afraid you'd say that…"

In the blink of an eye, he snatched me off my feet and hoisted me into the air like a rolled-up carpet. He had some serious muscles for a dead guy!

"NOOO!" I shouted. "Put me down!"

"I'm sorry, Spark, but it's the only way. In you go, then!"

Without any further delay, he plopped me down into the toxic goo.

SPLOOORP.

It felt like I'd been tossed into cold beef stew! Muck filled up my clothes in an instant. Glop squished between my armpits and sloshed between my toes. Bat bones and rat teeth poked me like little knives.

"Creeping cripes!" I shouted.

The fumes from the stew were so bad they were making my head spin.

"I've got something that'll help with the stink!" Caledonia said.

She raced over to a shelf and took down a jar of moldy mushrooms. She opened the lid and pulled out two small ones. Then she hurried back and knelt in front of me.

"Just bear with me, Sparky…"

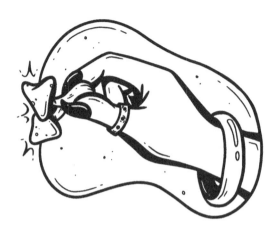

With two quick flicks of her thumbs, she popped one up each of my nostrils. I had to gasp through my mouth for breath.

"*I dode wud mudrooms id my node!*"

"Trust me, Sparky. You'll thank me for it," she said.

There was a loud clanking out in the Pit, like a school bell ringing. I could hear feet trampling on the walkway, voices growling loudly.

"Ooh, the workday's over," Caledonia said. "The tavern will be filling up for Grumpy Hour soon. I'd better get to the counter!"

She stood up and went dashing for the door.

The Big Whiff

Just before she disappeared, Caledonia called back over her shoulder.

"Good luck, Sparky! If you make it back, I'll stand you up to another pepper soda!"

Then she was gone. And it was just Fetrol and me.

"We really shouldn't delay any longer," he said. "I want them to find you as soon as possible…"

"Want *who* to find me?"

"*Murkles*," Fetrol said. "The people who work in the Big Whiff. Between you and me, young Spark, they're fishy folk all around. They do things quite backward down there. You'll do best not to offend them, understand?"

I shook my head.

"Not really…"

"Righty-o, then. *Ta-ta!*"

"Wait!" I shouted.

But Fetrol reached up and grabbed the chain hanging above the muckbucket. He gave it one yank, and the floor just seemed to open up beneath my feet.

The next thing I knew, I was hurtling downward. Surrounded by a hundred gallons of the Shakylegs' nastiest leftovers!

5. Down the Tubes

It was like I'd been sucked down a huge drain.

I bounced through twists and turns in the pipe like a wad of scum. My elbows and knees got banged and bruised. My head got rattled. I gasped, only to receive a huge mouthful of fish-flavored slop!

Down, down, down...

I seemed to tumble like this for minutes. Just when I was beginning to think I might suffocate, the pipe suddenly opened up below me.

I cannonballed down into a pool of rancid goop.

"AAAGGHHH!"

Splooosh.

I was completely submerged for a moment. I fought my way to the surface, kicking for everything I was worth. Then I burst through a layer of film, spitting and retching.

"Blech! Blech! Blech!"

I looked around to find I was in some sort of grimy lake—but it was full of rotten kitchen scraps! Apple cores and bat wings bobbed by. Maggots wriggled and writhed. Big black flies zipped over the surface like missiles.

Even worse, more garbage kept falling out of holes in the ceiling! I looked up just in time to see a tube gurgle and barf out a spout of fresh slop.

BURRBBLLRBLOOORP.

I barely avoided getting hit by this vomit blast.

"Good grief!" I said. "This place is awful!"

Somehow, Caledonia's mushrooms were still in my nose. They were blocking out most of the stench, but odors still trickled in. It smelled like eggs and meat left out in the sun for weeks.

I have to get out of here! I thought frantically.

The problem was, there didn't seem to be a way out.

The pond seemed to spread endlessly in

every direction. I spun around, treading scum, searching through the gloom with my eyes…

There!

I spotted a big rock sticking up from the edge of a stone riverbank. It was the only solid ground in sight. I didn't think twice. With a burst of energy, I started swimming for it.

I pulled like an Olympian, stroking for everything I was worth. But swimming in toxic slop is no easy task! Green and brown sludge clung to my clothes, weighing me down. Fish skeletons emerged and dipped before my eyes. It was enough to drive a guy crazy!

I just gritted my teeth and paddled harder.

By the time I reached the edge, I was so exhausted I was seeing double. I dragged myself up onto the rocks and clung there, dazed, with the wretched goop dripping off me.

"If I ever see Fetrol again…I'm flushing him down…the troll toilet," I gasped.

I flopped over onto my back and gazed mindlessly at the darkness above me.

To my surprise, the darkness was gazing back!

"What the…?"

Two wet, black eyes were staring down at me. They were set in an ugly green face with big catfish lips and fleshy gills. I was about to scream, but before I could utter a sound, the face spoke.

"*Whooo?*"

The word was burbly. Like someone speaking through a clogged pipe.

"W-w-who *what?*" I said, petrified.

The big catfish lips moved again.

"Who *you?*"

"I'm S-spark."

"Mmm...Spark."

I scrambled backward and sat up.

The creature standing in front of me was long and slippery and scaly, like a frog crossed with a fish. He had on grimy pants, and he was carrying a wrench in his webbed fingers. A fin stuck up from the top of his head.

"Why you here?" the creature asked in his weird, gurgling voice.

"Thoracks sent me," I replied.

The creature blinked and cocked his head to the side. If he knew who Thoracks was, he didn't give me any sign.

"Are you a m-murkle?" I asked.

The creature nodded once.

"Okay then...what's your name?"

A *ribbit* sound escaped the back of his throat. It sounded sort of like *Glub*.

"Uhh. Nice to meet you...Glub," I said.

"Mmm," Glub replied.

The Big Whiff

We sat there in silence as I dripped sludge and grease. The toxic lake bubbled and farted behind me. Yet another batch of slop splattered down in the distance.

I was starting to wonder if we would stay here and have a staring contest all afternoon. But then, without another word, Glub turned and began walking away.

I perked up.

"Am I supposed to follow you?" I asked.

"Mmm," Glub said.

I guess that means yes…

Uncertainly, I rose to my feet and set off after him. I didn't know where we were going. But I was all too happy to leave the lake of rancid muckbucket scraps far behind!

6. Murkletown

I followed Glub's slippery shape as he wandered through a jumble of mossy boulders. I finally had a chance to look around the place a bit.

So, this is the Big Whiff...

It looked like a cross between a sewer and a cave. The walls were dripping wet, and a weird green fog hung over everything like a swamp. Centipedes and lizards slithered over the rocks around us.

Caledonia's mushrooms were still doing their job keeping the smell out. But I could tell the stench hadn't improved, even with the gross lake far behind. I tried to just breathe through my mouth.

"Where are we going?" I panted.

"See Plop," Glub said.

"Who's Plop?"

"The Big Glurt. He run things down here."

"Oh," I said. "*Great.*"

I've never done well with authority figures. They don't mix well with my lively spirit. But I figured I would just have to turn on the old charm when the time came.

It got really dark for a while as we walked. The eerie glow in the air dimmed, and I was having a hard time seeing where I was going. I had to follow the sound of Glub's wet feet slapping in the darkness.

Just when I thought I might lose track of him altogether, I began to see torchlight shining up ahead. I could hear more murkle voices too. *Lots* of them.

We turned another corner, and suddenly we were standing in front of what looked like a whole village!

Huts made of rock and mud were jumbled together. Dozens of murkles were ducking in and out of them, carrying tools and bundles. Their gurgly voices croaked and called out to each other through the gloom.

"Woah," I whispered. "Murkletown…"

Glub plodded ahead.

"Come on," he said. "You late."

How could I be late if nobody knew I was coming? I wondered.

But I was starting to realize that asking Glub questions was sort of pointless. So, I just followed along.

We walked straight up one of the muddy,

crowded streets. Right off the bat, murkles began staring at me like I was something nasty Glub had dragged in on a string. They whispered in their croaky voices.

"Glub got a brunt…"

"Where he find that thing?"

"Don't touch it. Got germs…"

Sheesh! I thought. *They sure don't make a guy feel welcome around here.*

I just tried to keep my head down and not draw attention to myself. But we had only gone a little way up the first street when a finger poked me in the side.

"Hey, watch it!" I said. "This isn't a petting zoo!"

I looked down to see two short murkles following along beside us. They were smaller than me, and their voices were squeaky. One had big front teeth poking out between his lips.

"Glub, where you get this brunt from?" he asked.

"Yeah. Why's he all covered in shmucky?" the other said.

Glub spun around and shooed them with his webbed fingers.

"Flap. Flop. Go away."

But the little murkles didn't go away. They slapped right along beside us, pinching my skin and poking at my clothes.

"Where your flappers?" the taller one asked.

"I don't have flappers. I have toes."

The shorter one pulled my hair in hard jerks.

"What's this? Brown moss?"

"Oww! That's hair, not moss. Let go!"

They shook their heads and chuckled madly.

"He sure ugly," the little one said.

"*Real* ugly," the big one agreed.

"Speak for yourself, you buck-toothed tadpole!"

I thought about yanking one of them by the silly blue fin on his head. See how he liked it! But we had suddenly stopped walking, and the crowd around us had grown silent.

We were standing in front of a huge hut with a seaweed curtain over the door. About a thousand fish bones decorated the walls, and there was an intimidating murkle with a spear standing guard outside.

"We here," Glub said. "Time to see Plop."

The guard pulled back the seaweed curtain and waved me in. I smoothed back my hair and adjusted my clothes. Mustering my dignity, I ducked through the curtain.

Better get this over with, I thought.

7. Plop

It was dim in the hut.

I had to wait for my eyes to adjust. But when they did, I got a shock. There was an enormous throne made of rusty pipes on the other side of the room. And sitting on this throne was the biggest murkle I'd seen yet!

He was huge and green, with a fat belly shining in the candlelight. The fin on his head was blood red, and he was wearing a gigantic bolt on a chain necklace.

Glub bowed his head.

"Big Glurt, I have brought you…"

Before he could even finish the sentence, though, Flap and Flop came bursting through the seaweed curtain.

"Uncle Plop! Look what Glub found!"

"It's an ugly brunt! Can we keep him?"

The big murkle waited for them to calm down. Then he stood up from his pipe throne, his big belly rolling. He must have been eight feet tall!

"Brunt? In the Big Whiff?" he said. "Must be some mistake. He fall in the toilet or something?"

The two little murkles laughed hysterically.

"Found him in the muck pond," Glub said.

"Mmm. Somebody *did* flush him then."

He crossed the room and looked down at me over his big belly. If I wasn't nervous before, I was now.

"How'd you get down here, brunt?" Plop asked.

"My name is *Spark*," I said. "And Throacks sent me down here."

"Thoracks? Why? You mess something up?"

My cheeks flushed. He'd hit the nail on the head! But I didn't let on that he was right. I just shrugged and played it cool.

"Guess he just thought you might need my help."

Plop squinted an eye at me.

"You know much about pipes?"

"Not really?" I admitted.

"How 'bout wrenches? You know wrenches?"

My eyes drifted.

"Ehh, I guess not…"

Plop crossed his flabby arms.

"You ever use a welder before?"

I could only shake my head sheepishly.

"No."

Plop let out a laugh that shook the seaweed curtain.

"You about as useful as *brrrbllgrrt*!" he shouted.

I had no idea what *brrrbllgrrt* was, but it sent the whole room into hysterics. The little murkles fell over each other guffawing. Even Glub let out a little burble of laughter.

Great! I thought. *Laughed at by a bunch of fish-toads!*

I plucked up my usual spirit.

"Thoracks sent me because I'm the best worker in Dungeonworld. The best anywhere. I'll outwork every murkle down here!"

"Oh yeah?" Plop said, sneering at my gusto. "I guess we see about that…*big, bad brunt.*"

He raised his hand like he was going to dismiss me. But something must have caught his eye. He bent down to look closely at my face.

"What's that?" he said.

"What's what?"

"There…in your nose?"

My nose?

I reached up and touched my nostrils. *The*

mushrooms. I'd forgotten all about them since we'd arrived in Murkletown.

"Oh," I said. "They're for the smell."

Plop's grin faded into a scowl.

"What smell? You say my village smell bad?"

He seemed to suddenly get taller. And *fatter.* I tried to double back on my comment.

"Of course not!" I said. "I'd never say that!"

"Well then. Take them out."

"Take…them…out?"

Plop nodded menacingly.

The absolute last thing I wanted to do was take Caledonia's mushrooms out of my nose. They were the only thing protecting me from the full force of the stench down here. But the Big Glurt's glare was too strong to deny. There was no getting out of this.

"S-sure thing," I muttered.

With trembling hands, I reached up and plucked the snotty mushrooms from my nose. My eyes instantly began to water a little.

"Take a deep breath," Plop said. "*Smell* the fresh air."

Bracing myself, I drew a teensy breath through my nose.

GREAT STINKING GADZOOKS!

It was worse than anything I could have imagined! Like a thousand rotting diapers pan-fried in toxic waste. It took every ounce of self-control I possessed not to start puking on the spot.

"Smell nice?" Plop asked.

I gazed at him through quivering tears.

"Lovely…" I managed.

He nodded, satisfied.

"Okay, brunt. Thoracks sent you to work? You work." He snapped his fingers. "Glub, take him with you."

Glub looked up, startled.

"Me…Big Glurt?"

"You found him. He your responsibility. Make him feel…*welcome*."

Glub didn't seem at all pleased about having to babysit me. But he clearly wasn't going to argue with Plop. So, he wrapped a wet, rubbery hand around my neck and steered me out of the room.

"Come!" he said.

It was good timing. I was about to pass out from the stench! As I ducked through the seaweed curtain, Plop called out in his thundering voice.

"You behave down here, brunt…or you just might get flushed again!"

Flap and Flop burst into cackling laughter once more. Then, the seaweed curtain closed.

8. The Pipeworks

OUTSIDE THE HUT, I struggled to breathe without passing out. The swamp fumes of the Big Whiff were strong enough to peel paint! I puffed and wheezed pitifully.

Glub just looked down at me like he wished the muck pond had swallowed me whole. He set his squishy jaw and jerked his head.

"Hurry," he said. "We almost late."

"Late for what?" I asked, hand on my belly.

"Work."

"But…the workday just finished!"

Glub pointed a bulby finger towards the rocky ceiling overhead.

"Up there, it finished. Down in the Big Whiff, workday just starting."

I recalled what Fetrol had said about murkles being sort of backward. I figured that this must have been what he was talking about. But I had already worked one day in the smithy, and it had gone horribly. I didn't want another one.

I was totally pooped!

I tried to give Glub a casual wave goodbye.

"In that case, I'll just let you get to it," I said. "I'm gonna rest up somewhere, and I'll be all fresh for tomorrow…"

Glub snagged me by the arm.

"Oh no! Big Glurt say you work…you work!"

Sheesh.

He pulled me right along. All I could do was moan and groan.

We joined a long line of bodies heading out of the village. Every murkle I saw was carrying wrenches, hammers, and hard hats. Even the little murkle kids were tagging along with buckets full of nuts and bolts.

"Where's everybody going?" I asked.

"The Pipeworks," Glub said.

What are the Pipeworks? I wondered.

But I didn't have to wonder for long. We had only walked about ten minutes when I began to hear what sounded like a train station up ahead. The rocky ceiling rose higher and higher. Suddenly, we were in a big, open chamber.

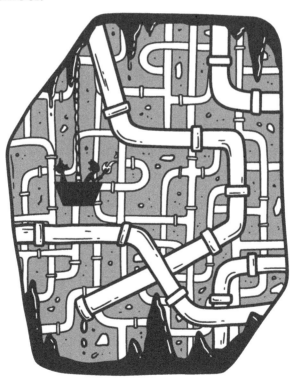

I craned my head back.

"Woooah....*Pipes*!"

There were pipes everywhere! A huge, tangled mess of pipes, all criss-crossing and zig-zagging every which way. It looked like a plumbing highway. The space was so big everything echoed like a giant cave.

CLANG. RING. BONG.

Murkles were already working up there. Their slippery shapes were climbing over pipes, turning wrenches, hoisting chains, and swinging hammers. Sparks flashed here and there where they were welding with fire.

Glub swelled with pride.

"Murkles keep the pipes working," he said. "Murkles are important!"

"I'll say," I told him. "What's in these pipes anyways?"

"*Brrrblllgrrt.*"

"I keep hearing that word," I told him. "What is...brrrblllgrrt?"

Glub looked at me like I was dense.

"You know what brrrblllgrrt is."

I pictured all of those toilets up there in the Pit just flushing away. Thousands of gallons of the worst stuff in Dungeonworld plummeting down here and whizzing through these tangled pipes overhead.

My stomach lurched.

"You're right," I gulped. "Murkles are *very* important."

Glub hitched up his grimy trousers.

"Time to start," he said.

He began walking towards a tall steel ladder mounted to the rocky wall. I followed along reluctantly.

"Where are we working?" I asked.

Glub aimed his bulby fingertip straight up towards the ceiling.

"The Lifter," he said.

I tilted my head back and stared into the greenish, dim light above us. Way, way up at the top, I could just see a crane perched on a rocky ledge.

I suddenly got a little burst of excitement.

"Wow, a crane?" I said. "Awesome! Let's go!"

Glub began climbing the steel ladder, and I followed up right behind him.

I suddenly wasn't tired anymore. Of all the crummy jobs I could have ended up with in the Big Whiff, working on a huge crane had to be the coolest!

9. The Lifter

UP AND UP we climbed, hopping from one steel ladder to another. At every level we passed, murkles were hard at work, calling out to one another in their weird voices.

"Loog, more pipe!"

"Turn the big valve twice, Twerp…"

"Tell Blub to bring the grease!"

We climbed right past them.

Soon we were so high that I started feeling a little dizzy. Just when I thought I would have to chicken out, we reached a rocky landing at the top of things. The crane was sitting at the edge like a giant metal flamingo.

My discomfort totally vanished.

"Cool!" I shouted.

I ran up to the huge piece of machinery, marveling at every little detail. The heavy steel treads. The enormous boxy engine. The long arm with the snapping steel claw dangling out in space.

Glub hopped into the cabin and settled into the cracked leather seat. He started flipping switches and adjusting levers. When he had everything set, he turned a key, and the whole machine came roaring to life.

VROOOOMMM.

It sounded like a monster truck revving! The crane pumped oily smoke from a pipe in the back. I jumped up onto the side and stared at the controls.

"This is great!" I shouted. "When do I get to try?"

Glub shooed me away.

"You don't try," he said.

"Then…what am I supposed to do?"

"Just watch."

"You kidding me? Plop said you were supposed to teach me!"

"Big Glurt told me take you with me," Glub said haughtily. "He didn't say nothing 'bout teaching."

"But…but…"

Before I could come up with an argument, Glub pulled down on a lever. The whole cab of the crane started to swing around. It almost bowled me over!

"Whoaaa!"

I jumped down and retreated to safety.

"Stay out the way," Glub shouted over the engine's roar. "I got important work to do."

He lowered the snapping claw down into the chasm below. Within moments, it was obvious he'd all but forgotten about me.

What a rip-off! I thought.

For the next several hours, I had no choice but to sit there and watch Glub work. It was a total bummer. Here I was, ready and able to do my part, and he wouldn't even let me try!

I kept making nasty faces at him. But he just hummed right along, cranking the crane levers and revving the engine. Eventually, I got tired of being moody and just parked my butt on the ground.

The Big Whiff

In the end, I had to admit, it was pretty cool to watch.

Glub worked the controls like he was playing a video game. He swung the big arm this way and that, picking up pipes with the big claw dangling from chains on the end. Murkles down below would signal what they wanted him to do, and Glub would get it done lickety-split.

Time drifted by...

My eyelids began to droop. My long day was catching up to me. I must have nodded off because when I woke up, everything had gone mysteriously quiet. The crane engine had been shut off.

I turned to see Glub climbing down from the cabin.

"What's going on?" I asked, rubbing my eyes.

"Have to go talk to the Big Glurt," he said. "Be back soon…"

He walked over to the ladder and began climbing down backward. He stopped at the top and gave me a stern frown.

"Don't touch Lifter!" he warned.

"Chill out, I won't!"

He watched me suspiciously for a moment, just to make sure his message had sunk in. I gave him my best innocent look. Satisfied, he continued to climb down.

I waited until he was far below.

"What I meant to say," I whispered, "is that I won't touch it *much...*"

I rose to my feet and dusted off my pants. Turning away from the ledge, I went tiptoeing towards the slumbering crane.

10. Flap and Flop

I CLIMBED UP THE side of the crane, plopped into the leather seat, and sat there looking at all the controls.

My turn to run the show! I thought giddily.

I tried touching the big joystick at the center, only to find it was still greasy from Glub's hand.

"Ewww!"

I used my dirty shirt to wipe it off. When it was clean, I wrapped my fingers around it again and twisted it experimentally. I pushed and pulled

the lever down by my hip that Glub had used to raise and lower the claw.

I had no intention of actually turning the thing on. But it felt good to sit in the driver's seat and pretend for a while. I was just about to get out when two voices nearby almost made me jump out of my skin.

"I dare you spit off the edge…"

"No, I dare *you!*"

I looked over to see Flap and Flop, the little murkles from earlier, come bounding up the ladder. They pointed at me with mouths hanging open.

"What are *you* doing up here?"

I pointed right back.

"What are *you two* doing up here?"

"What's it look like?" the short one said. "*Snooping.*"

I hadn't forgotten about all the poking and prodding they had done earlier. I gave them the cold shoulder.

"Well, little kids aren't supposed to be up here. Get lost."

"Brunts aren't supposed to be in the Big Whiff," Flop retorted. "So, you get lost!"

"I'm not going anywhere," I told him.

"Neither are we!"

To my total annoyance, they climbed right up on the side of the crane and stuck their slimy green faces into the cabin.

"Wow! Look at all the flickers!" Flap said.

He reached in and tried to touch the switches. I swatted his oily hand.

"Don't touch that! This is way too important for you."

"Says who?"

"Says me!"

"You just a brunt. You not even allowed to *use* the Lifter."

"Yes, I am!" I said. "Glub spent all day teaching me."

"*Pbbbt!* You probably don't even know how to turn it on," Flop said.

"Uh, you just turn this key here, genius."

I pointed to the tarnished silver key in the dash panel.

Flap gave me a challenging look.

"Do it then."

I wanted to thump him right between his oily eyes! I've never liked spoiled brats, especially ones who get special treatment because they have an important uncle. But I wasn't about to cave in to his peer pressure.

"I don't feel like it," I said.

"Yeah, right. You too scared."

That *really* got me going.

If there's one thing I can't stand, it's being called a chicken.

"I'm not scared of anything!" I told him.

"Prove it then. Turn the Lifter on."

I sat there stewing with anger. I could think of about a million reasons not to cave in and do what he said. But I had an overwhelming urge just to wipe that smug grin off his fishy face.

My vengeful side got the better of me.

"Fine!" I said. "Step back."

I wrapped my fingers around the little silver key. Pushing back all the worries I had about why this was such a dumb idea, I gave it a twist.

VRROOOM!

The crane's motor roared to life beneath me! I could feel the horsepower as the cabin shook and rumbled. It made me a little nervous.

"There," I shouted. "I turned it on. You happy?"

I reached for the little key and was just about

to turn it off again. But Flop darted his hand toward the controls.

"Whooee! Let me try…"

He wrapped his webbed digits around the joystick and jerked it. The whole cabin started to swing.

"Woah, stop it!" I shouted.

I tried to break his grip. But then Flap latched on as well.

"No, I want to try!"

He shifted the joystick again. The cabin swung wildly back the other way. Things quickly evolved into a wrestling match for the controls.

"Knock it off!" I said. "I'm serious!"

The engine roared as the crane pivoted back and forth. The heavy steel claw hanging from the long chains began to swing like a wrecking ball. Before I could regain control, the claw banged hard against an enormous pipe down below

KLOOONG.

I watched in horror as a section of the pipe broke like an eggshell. A torrent of brown liquid came spewing out. Thousands of gallons gushed into the air like a fountain!

We stopped fighting and gawked at it…

Please, please let that be dirty water, I thought desperately.

But it was only a matter of moments before a horrible smell hit my nose. A smell too awful to mistake.

"Oh no," I gagged. "It's not water, it's… it's…"

Flap and Flop let out bloodcurdling screams. "BRRRBLLLGRRT!"

11. Brrrblllgrrt Flood

I COULDN'T BELIEVE THIS. Just hours before, I had caused a giant, watery flood at the blacksmith's shop. But this flood was worse. *Far* worse. There was no easy way to put it. We had just caused a huge flood of…

Monster poop.

I gazed in horror as it poured out of the enormous, broken pipe like a brown geyser. It went sloshing and crashing through the pipes below and splashed down onto the floor like a wave.

GLOOOSH!

Flap, Flop, and I could only watch as the lumpy tide went sweeping through the chasm like a river. Murkles everywhere were suddenly yelling and screaming.

"Brrrblllgrrt flood!"

"Everybody off the floor!"

"Climb, climb, climb!"

Their slender shapes began clambering up the walls and clinging to pipes. They looked like lizards climbing a riverbank as they helped each other to higher ground.

I was gripped with panic.

"I can't believe this!" I screeched. "Is everyone okay down there?"

"I think so," Flop answered anxiously. "Nobody stays on the floor during workday."

He seemed to be right. Everywhere I looked, murkles were already huddled safely on higher ledges. Nobody was calling out for salvation from the brown flood sweeping through the Pipeworks. But the situation was still far from being under control.

"We have to stop it somehow!" I shouted.

The cowardly little murkles, however, had seen enough.

"I'm out of here!" Flap said.

"Me too!" Flop agreed.

They leaped down from the cabin and ran for it.

I bellowed after them.

"You jerks! This is all your fault!"

They weren't listening, though. They headed straight for the ladder and shimmied down at top speeds.

Which left me all alone to sort things out…

There has to be some way to stop this flood, I thought frantically.

But how?!

There was no magic valve I could turn to make it shut off. No wrench big enough to fix this problem. The pipe was just broken. And it would keep gushing unless somebody could…

"Plug it up," I mumbled.

An idea formed in my head suddenly. I wasn't even sure it would work. But I knew I had to try, and I was the only person in a position to do something.

Making up my mind quickly, I scooted up in the seat and began searching the rocky ledges beneath me. I tried to ignore the churning sewage far below as my eyes went hunting for something just the right shape…

A-ha!

I saw a boulder the size of an armchair nestled in a cleft just beneath me. It would have to do.

Fighting back a flutter of nerves, I turned the silver key again. The crane engine screamed to life, puffing out smoke.

VROOOM!

My fingers twitched and wriggled as I grabbed the joystick. I had watched Glub maneuver this thing all day. I was pretty sure I knew how it worked, but there was only one way to find out.

"You can do this, Spark," I told myself.

Biting my tongue between my teeth, I pushed the joystick to the left. The arm went swinging over, carrying the chain and heavy claw with it. I was careful to keep it under control this time. I stopped when it was directly above the boulder.

Now for the tricky part…

I reached down and pulled the lever next to my hip. The claw began to descend slowly on the chain.

Clink. Clink. Clink.

I waited for it to stop swinging, just like I'd seen Glub do all day. When it was totally still, I tapped the little red button on the lever. The claw dropped.

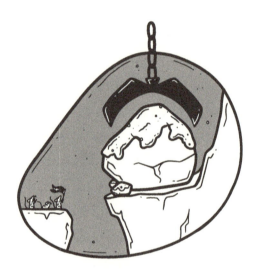

Clomp.

It snapped shut on the boulder.

"Bingo!" I shouted.

With the claw secure, I pushed the lever up and nudged the joystick to the right. The engine struggled and groaned. Slowly, the boulder rose into the air.

I brought it right up until it was level with my eye. Using every ounce of control I possessed, I swung the boulder over and positioned it just above the gushing hole in the pipe. Saying a little prayer, I tapped the red button again.

The claw snapped open.

THUNK!

The boulder plopped right down into the hole. Like a faucet had just been turned off, the brown goo stopped gushing. Only a tiny trickle seethed out through the cracks around the rock.

I sagged back in the cracked leather seat.

"Thank goodness…"

There was no time to celebrate, though. Feet were suddenly slapping through the dust on the ground beside me. I looked over to see Glub running my way.

His eyes were furious.

"I told you not to touch the Lifter!"

"It wasn't me!" I tried to tell him.

But he wasn't hearing any excuses. He jumped up, grabbed me by the arm, and yanked me headfirst out of the cabin.

"Save it for the Big Glurt!" he said.

He dragged me across the ledge and sent me scrambling down the ladder. I had no choice but to descend into the horrible odor rising up from below.

12. The Wrench of Shame

The long climb down seemed to take forever, especially with Glub stomping my fingers with his webbed feet.

"Hurry up!" he barked.

"Oww! I'm trying!"

The only relief I had was discovering that I must have capped the pipe at just the right moment. By the time we reached the bottom, most of the brown flood was gone. Only a stinking ooze was left on the ground. Murkles were spraying everything down with hoses.

Ugh! Smells like sewage churned in a blender!

A crowd was waiting for us at the bottom. Hundreds of murkles watched with angry eyes and clenched fists as we stepped down off the ladder. They made a tight circle around me.

"Crazy brunt! You filled the whole place with brrrblllgrrt…"

"Could have drowned us all!"

"Never should have come here in the first place!"

I tried once again to defend myself, but I couldn't get a word in with all the screaming and yelling. Things only quieted down when

Plop came forcing his way through the crowd with a murderous look on his scaly face.

"How'd this happen?" Plop said. "Who's responsible?"

Glub shoved me forward angrily.

"It was him, Big Glurt! He switched on the Lifter when I wasn't looking. He knocked a hole in the big pipe!"

"No, I didn't!" I argued. "Those two did it… Flap and Flop!"

I pointed to the two little murkles standing behind Plop with mock innocent looks on their faces.

Flop gestured wildly.

"It wasn't us, Uncle Plop! The silly brunt was already in the Lifter when we found him. He turned it on all by himself!"

"This true?" Plop said.

"Well, yes…but they were egging me on! And then they grabbed the controls and smashed the pipe! If I hadn't blocked up the hole with that rock, it would still be pumping out stinky brown—"

"SILENCE!" Plop shouted.

I shut my mouth.

"You should never have touched the Lifter," he said. "And you, Glub…you should never have turned your back on a sneaky brunt!"

Glub bowed his head.

"Sorry, Big Glurt…"

Plop's big belly shook and rippled with rage.

"This muck-up is unforgivable!"

He turned his bulk my way, towering over me.

"What are you going to do?" I asked meekly.

"What I should have done when I first saw you," Plop said. "I'm sending you right back where you come from! But first…you get the Wrench of Shame."

The murkles gasped.

"*Wrench of Shame*," they whispered.

Plop held out his flabby hand. Somebody slapped an enormous wrench down onto his palm, and he came striding forward. I thought for sure he was going to clobber me with it! But instead, he did something even scarier…

He held the wrench beneath my chin. There was a shriek of bending metal as the muscles in his green arms flexed. Suddenly, the wrench was wrapped around my neck like a bowtie!

"Yikes!" I shouted.

Plop stepped back and dusted his hands.

"When Thoracks see that," he said, "he'll grind up your bones like pepper. Now, toss this brunt into the Pump!"

Strong, webby hands gripped my arms. They

dragged me towards a big, black machine sitting against the chasm wall. Two murkles were already waiting there. They turned a wheel-shaped handle on the side. A bolt clicked, and a small hatch swung open.

I stood looking at the dark hole inside.

"Can we discuss this?" I asked.

"Throw him in!" Plop replied.

I got a kick in the rump, and through the hatch I went.

"Oof!"

I landed in a wet, cold puddle in the dark. I spun around to find a crowd of enraged murkles staring at me through the hatchway. Plop's squishy jaw was twitching.

"Tell Thoracks never send another brunt down here again," he said. "Or else!"

I tried to think of something I could say to make the situation better. Some apology that would fix the damage I had helped cause. But the hatch was already closing, and the time for apologies seemed long gone.

The last glimpse I got before the door shut

completely was of Flap and Flop smiling at me with their evil little faces. They wriggled their sticky fingers.

"Bye, brunt!"

Then the door closed, and I was in total darkness.

"You spoiled fishy brats!" I shouted

My angry voice just bounced off the dark, metal walls around me.

Somewhere nearby, a valve creaked. The tank began slowly filling up with icy cold water. It rose above my shins, then my knees. The icy tide engulfed my stomach, chest, and neck. When it began to cover my head, I cried out in terror.

"Help! I'm gonna drown in here!"

But help didn't come...

Instead, there was a loud flushing sound all around me. The pressure in the tank seemed to

change, and I got sucked straight upward like a bubble in a straw.

13. Flushed Again

Things got sort of hazy after that.

I remember tumbling and bouncing through pipes, clonking my head on a hundred steel turns.

My arms and legs got yanked in thousand different directions. All in all, it was a lot like my trip down the muckbucket. Except, this time, I had a stupid wrench wrapped around my neck!

Just when I thought I couldn't hold my breath a moment longer, I came bursting out of the pipe in a geyser of water.

Splooosh!

I landed headfirst on a rocky floor and lay there coughing and hacking.

"Ugh," I choked. "I'm never going down a waterslide again..."

I waited for my head to stop spinning, then looked around. I was back in the kitchen of the Shakylegs.

Somehow, the murkles had sent me right back up through the muckbucket! I tried to figure out how they could have managed this, but the answer was beyond me. I just rose unsteadily to my feet, wrung out my shirt, and went straggling through the swinging door.

"Caledonia, I'm back," I murmured. "I might need to take you up on that pepper soda..."

It was too loud in the tavern for anyone to hear me, though. Accordion music was blaring. Rough troll voices were shouting and singing. The two-headed dog was howling in the corner.

Fetrol was sitting at the counter eating a plate of wriggling brown noodles. He slurped one up greedily, then noticed me standing there in the doorway. His eyes swelled up like ostrich eggs.

"Oh, dear me," he said, wiping sauce off his chin. "This is not good."

"Sparky!" Caledonia shouted. "You're back soon, ain't you?"

I folded my hands behind my back.

"Yeah…I sort of had another rough day, Cal."

"Really? What happened?"

"Well, there was a little accident with the crane down there. A pipe or two might have exploded, and…"

Caledonia gasped.

"So, *that's* what sent the plumbing all woozy? The whole Pit's been having problems. Someone got sucked down a toilet just up the way!" She squinted at me closely. "What's that you got hanging under your chin?"

I touched the twisted wrench around my neck.

"The murkles put it on me," I said. "They called it the—"

"Wrench of Shame," Fetrol interrupted. "This is bad, young Spark. Very bad."

"What's the big deal?" I told him. "It's just a wrench!"

Honestly, I felt like I'd gotten off easy. All I had to do was find someone to help pry this heavy thing off me. But Fetrol didn't seem to agree.

"The Wrench of Shame is not just any wrench. It's a symbol! It means that you have offended the murkles beyond forgiveness." He shook his head and tisked. "When Thoracks sees that, he'll have no choice but to punish you."

"Like, how?" I asked nervously.

Fetrol touched a finger to his scabby chin.

"If I remember correctly, the last fellow who came up with the Wrench of Shame around his neck was dipped in sugar and fed to cockroaches."

"Yipes! Help me get it off, then!"

"No can do," Fetrol said. "Thoracks will hear about it one way or another. He might even be on his way up here right now."

Caledonia thumped me on the back.

"You might be better off just flushing yourself back down the troll toilet, Sparky."

"Thanks a lot, Cal," I grumbled.

Fetrol sighed and put his napkin down.

"I'd better take you to his office right away," he said. "And I was thoroughly enjoying my plate of worm pasta. Oh well…come along, young man!"

I knew that if I argued, Fetrol would

probably just pick me up and throw me over his shoulder. I was too tired for that nonsense. I just ducked under the counter and let him collar me.

"Good luck, Sparky," Caledonia called. "If the roaches leave much of you, come back around to see me!"

Once again, we passed right by my little yellow-curtained notch out in the walkway. And, once again, Fetrol wouldn't even stop to let me catch some rest.

"Oh no! If I turn you loose with that wrench wrapped around your neck, I'll be the one dipped in sugar! Just hurry along now..."

Really, it was probably a good idea to keep moving. Everywhere we went, I saw signs of the plumbing disaster I had caused down in the Big Whiff.

Cruddy water was leaking out from under doorways. A sink was gushing like a fountain in a ghoul soda shop. The citizens of Dungeon-world were in a high state of anger.

"**If I find the squirt what did this,**" a passing troll complained, "**I'll make toe jelly outta him!**"

I put my head down and kept right on walking.

We managed to make it to Thorack's office in one piece. Fetrol stepped aside.

"All right, in you go then…"

"Aren't you coming with me?" I asked.

Fetrol held up a clammy hand.

"I have a stomach full of fresh worm pasta, don't I? The last thing I want to see is a cockroach feeding frenzy!"

I sighed.

"Whatever..."

I knocked timidly on the door. There was a muffled reply from within. With one final sour look at Fetrol, I turned the knob and entered.

14. Colonel Crank

I slipped into the office and shut the door quietly behind me. To my surprise, I wasn't bonked on the head right away. Nobody even yelled or screamed at me. Instead, things looked...*calm*.

Thoracks was sitting behind his desk, tapping his clawed fingertips together. Next to him stood a short goblin wearing a crisp uniform. He had a little circle of glass in his eye and a baton under his arm.

They were both gazing at me intently.

"Sooo, I'm back," I said. "Haha..."

Thoracks just glared at me with a weird little smile on his bullish face. Eventually, he rose to his feet, walked across the room, and reached toward me with his big, blue paws.

Here it comes! I thought.

But he didn't wallop me into oblivion. Instead, he grabbed the bent wrench around my neck. With a mighty jerk, he pried the two ends apart.

CREEEAAAK!

The wrench came free like a silk handkerchief. Thoracks tossed it into the hay pile in the corner, then stepped aside politely.

"He's all yours, Colonel Crank."

Now, it was the little goblin's turn to come striding forward. He whapped the baton across his raspy palm, looking me up and down.

"So, you're the brunt who blew up the smithy?"

I tried not to look guilty, but there didn't seem to be much of a point.

"Yes, sir," I replied.

"Mm-hmm. And, you're also the one responsible for causing a sewage flood in the Big Whiff this evening?"

That one hurt a bit worse. I lowered my eyes.

"Pretty much…"

Colonel Crank smiled maliciously.

"Well, maggot, it's clear to me that you're in need of an attitude adjustment!"

He poked me in the stomach with his baton, then whapped me on the spine.

"Suck in that gut! Straighten that back!"

"Owww!"

My back straightened. My belly flattened. My cheeks twitched with pain as I stared at the irate little goblin.

"Not so tough now, are you?" he said, smirking.

He turned back to Thoracks.

"I reckon this one will do just fine, governor."

Thoracks was really grinning now. He rubbed his big blue paws together and let out a growling throaty laugh.

"What's going on?" I blurted out. "What does he mean 'I'll do fine?'"

"After this last stunt you pulled in the Big Whiff," Thoracks said, "I thought for sure I'd have to feed you to the cockroaches. But the Colonel here heard about it, and he told me there was a place for you in the special forces... with the roughest, toughest monsters in all of Dungeonworld!"

The words he was saying slowly sunk in.

"Wait, are you telling me..."

"That's right," Thoracks beamed. "You're in the Army now!"

THE END

Made in the USA
Las Vegas, NV
13 July 2022